PUFFIN BOOKS

Sky Horses
The Whispering Tree

The third book in the quartet

Linda Chapman lives in Leicestershire with her family and two Bernese mountain dogs. When she is not writing, she spends her time looking after her two young daughters and baby son, horse riding and talking to people about writing.

You can find out more about Linda on her websites at *lindachapman.co.uk* and *lindachapmanauthor.co.uk*

Books by Linda Chapman

BRIGHT LIGHTS

CENTRE STAGE

MY SECRET UNICORN series

NOT QUITE A MERMAID series

SKY HORSES series

STARDUST series

UNICORN SCHOOL series

LINDA CHAPMAN

Sky Horses

The Whispering Tree

Illustrated by Ann Kronheimer

PUFFIN

PUFFIN BOOKS

Published by the Penguin Group
Penguin Books Ltd, 80 Strand, London WC2R ORL, England
Penguin Group (USA) Inc., 375 Hudson Street, New York, New York 10014, USA
Penguin Group (Canada), 90 Eglinton Avenue East, Suite 700, Toronto, Ontario, Canada M4P 2Y3
(a division of Pearson Penguin Canada Inc.)
Penguin Ireland, 25 St Stephen's Green, Dublin 2, Ireland (a division of Penguin Books Ltd)
Penguin Group (Australia), 250 Camberwell Road, Camberwell, Victoria 3124, Australia
(a division of Pearson Australia Group Pty Ltd)
Penguin Books India Pvt Ltd, 11 Community Centre, Panchsheel Park, New Delhi – 110 017, India
Penguin Group (NZ), 67 Apollo Drive, Rosedale, North Shore 0632, New Zealand
(a division of Pearson New Zealand Ltd)
Penguin Books (South Africa) (Pty) Ltd, 24 Sturdee Avenue, Rosebank,
Johannesburg 2196, South Africa

Penguin Books Ltd, Registered Offices: 80 Strand, London WC2R ORL, England

puffinbooks.com

First published 2009
1

Text copyright © Linda Chapman, 2009
Illustrations copyright © Ann Kronheimer, 2009
All rights reserved

The moral right of the author and illustrator has been asserted

Set in Bembo 15/22pt
Typeset by Palimpsest Book Production Limited, Grangemouth, Stirlingshire
Made and printed in England by Clays Ltd, St Ives plc

British Library Cataloguing in Publication Data
A CIP catalogue record for this book is available from the British Library

ISBN: 978-0-141-32332-9

www.greenpenguin.co.uk

To Fiona Ambery for first suggesting hagstones – and to Charlotte, Bea and Damaris. I hope you enjoy reading about the sky horses.

When the dark one returns, the door shall be reopened
And danger will threaten all living below.
If the binding is broken, they can be protected,
But one coming willingly lets the dark's power grow
Until the first gateway is split by magic
And he who is trapped is free to go.

Two gateways now balance the light and the darkness,
One lost in memory, hidden by the sea.
The dark door is reserved for the hand that creates it.
The other lies close to a whispering tree,
Deep underground and made from moonlight.
When it is found, then two can be free.

Yet danger is found with the new gateway —
Beware the dark horse who leaps for the sky.
With arrow of fire and grey feather's direction,
Two must help here or all hopes will die.
If the darkest impostor is not defeated,
Then never again will the cloud stallion fly.

Watching . . .

It was midnight. The wind swept through the trees outside the large house on the cliff top. Branches of a tree brushed against the window of the study, like bony fingers scraping at the glass. A woman with long blonde hair, Marianne, was sitting at the desk inside the study. Ignoring the sound, she stared at the grey stone in her hands. It had a single round hole through its centre.

'Two gateways,' she murmured. 'One hidden.'

She passed a hand over the stone. The air in the room seemed to shiver slightly. Marianne leant forward, seeing a picture forming in the centre of the stone. The picture grew bigger – a cliff with trees at the top. The cliff face was steep, covered in grass with gashes of bare soil. At the bottom of the cliff were jagged rocks that were covered with damp seaweed. Water glittered in pools between them.

A person came into the vision. A slim teenage girl, a younger version of Marianne, came scrambling down the cliff. She was wearing a long brown skirt, a shawl and old-fashioned boots and her blonde hair was blowing around her face. She paused as she came to a ledge of rock jutting out near the base of the cliffs.

'A gateway lost in memory,' Marianne whispered.

Another girl appeared in the vision. Marianne's eyes hardened. The second girl had the same honey-blonde hair and blue eyes, but her face was more heart-shaped. She looked about a year older and very determined. As she came

down the cliff, she started arguing
angrily with the girl at the bottom who
just laughed, tossed her hair back and
clambered over the ledge, before
disappearing beneath it.

Marianne chuckled to herself. 'Yes.
It was hidden well then and still is now.
But enough with the past. Let me see
the present.' She closed her fingers over
the hole in the stone and the picture
disappeared. 'Reveal the sky stallion,'
she whispered.

She opened her fingers and a new
vision formed, revealing a snow-white
stallion and a grey colt standing in a
clearing in the woods next to two
girls. The moon shone down on them.
The foal had a fluffy mane and a
mischievous expression. The stallion's

mane and tail swept to the floor; his
dark eyes were wise, his head noble.
There was something almost
otherworldly about both horses; the
lines of their bodies seemed hazy, as if
a fine mist surrounded them.

One of the girls had dark-brown
curls, laughing hazel eyes and skin the
colour of milk chocolate, but Marianne
barely even glanced at her. Her

attention was fixed on the tall, slim girl with long dark-blonde hair and a heart-shaped face. She was holding a stone with a hole in the centre.

'I am sure you think you can stop me just like she did . . .' As Marianne spoke, the blonde girl broke off from talking and glanced around uneasily. Her fingers tightened on a stone in her own hand and Marianne's vision vanished.

'But not this time,' Marianne hissed. 'Nothing will stop me this time . . .'

CHAPTER
One

'Wakey, wakey!'

Erin heard a voice and felt something tickling her nose. Still half asleep, she brushed it away.

'Erin!'

Erin opened her eyes. Chloe was leaning over her, stroking her nose with the tail of a cuddly toy horse. Erin giggled. 'Stop it!' she said, pushing her away.

'I thought you were never going to

wake up,' Chloe complained. 'I've been up for ages.'

Erin yawned. For a long time after she and Chloe had got back from the woods, she hadn't been able to sleep, and had lain in bed thinking about Tor, the magnificent sky stallion they had been talking to that evening. It was very weird to think that just a few weeks ago she'd had no idea that sky horses existed and now she and Chloe were trying to help one of them. Sky horses lived in the clouds – their moods and movements changed the weather. When the sky horses were quiet and peaceful, the weather was calm; when they were agitated, the wind and rain blew and when they fought there were storms.

Tor was the leader of the sky horses along the Dorset coastline. He and his young son, Mistral, had been captured by a dark spirit called Marianne. The girls were trying to help the horses get back to their kingdom in the clouds. But it wasn't proving to be easy. Erin rubbed her tired eyes and lay back down.

'Oh no! You are *not* going back to

sleep again,' Chloe declared, yanking the duvet off Erin's bed. 'If you go back to sleep, we'll be late getting to the stables this morning.'

Of course! Erin realized. *We're going riding today!* The thought of going to Hawthorn Stables acted like a magic spell, instantly sweeping her tiredness away. She jumped straight up and quickly started emptying out her rucksack, looking for her jodhpurs. 'What are you waiting for?' she teased, glancing at Chloe's surprised face. 'Do you have to be so slow?'

Chloe grinned and threw the cuddly horse at her.

'It took me ages to get to sleep last night,' Erin admitted as they both started to get dressed. 'I kept thinking about Tor and then about Marianne. Don't you think it's weird that we haven't seen her since we freed Mistral? It's almost two weeks now.'

'I know,' agreed Chloe. 'I'd have thought she'd have been trying to do something to us — capture Mistral again or something — but it's like she's vanished.'

Erin hesitated. 'A few times this week I've had this kind of prickling feeling, as if someone's watching me. I felt it again last night. I think she might be spying on us with magic.'

'Why didn't you say something to Tor?' asked Chloe, looking alarmed.

Erin shrugged. 'I wasn't sure about it. It was only when we got back that I kept remembering it.'

'You'd better tell Tor tonight. I hope it's not Marianne.' Chloe shivered. 'And I wish we knew why she's being so quiet.'

Erin's eyes met hers. 'It feels like she's waiting for something.'

'Chloe! Erin!' Chloe's mum called up the stairs, interrupting the girls' worried silence. 'Time for breakfast.'

Chloe went to the door. 'Coming, Mum!' She turned to Erin and spoke quickly. 'Look, we'd better not talk about it now – we don't want Mum and Dad to hear.'

Erin nodded. Chloe was right. No one was supposed to know about Tor or their magic. 'OK, later.'

'Later,' Chloe agreed.

The two girls started talking loudly

about the ponies at the riding school as they quickly finished getting dressed. Packing her nightdress away, Erin thought how lucky she was to have Chloe to share everything with. It felt like they had known each other forever.

In fact, they had first met just under a month ago on the day Erin had discovered that there were sky horses and that she was a stardust spirit – a special kind of person who could fly and do magic at night time. Stardust spirits were supposed to use their magic to look after nature. Chloe was a stardust spirit too. She'd turned into one for the first time just a few days before Erin. They'd agreed to start meeting up and had been best friends ever since.

They were both pony-mad and
longed for their own ponies. Chloe,
who had just moved into the area, had
started going to Hawthorn Stables like
Erin, which meant that they got to
hang out together at weekends, in school
holidays and on the days after school
when they persuaded their parents to
let them go to the stables to help.

When the girls were dressed, they hurried downstairs. Chloe's mum and dad were in the kitchen drinking coffee and reading the papers.

'Morning, you two,' said Chloe's dad, Mike, with a cheerful smile.

Erin could never get over how calm and quiet Chloe's house was. She had three older stepbrothers, and breakfast at her house was always very noisy. She usually just tried to read a book and ignore them all.

'So what are you going to be doing today at the stables?' asked Nicky, Chloe's mum.

'We're going on a beach ride,' replied Erin. Nicky had ridden lots herself when she was growing up and she loved talking about horses and riding.

'And let me guess: you'll be hoping you ride Kestrel?' said Nicky.

Erin grinned and nodded. Kestrel was a new pony at the stables, but already he was her favourite. He was a part-Arab grey and very lively. For a while, Erin had been scared of riding him, but now she loved him. She always tried to be the one to catch him and groom him if she could. Secretly, in her own head – and she didn't even tell Chloe this – she sometimes pretended that he was her very own pony.

'I bet you will get to ride him,' said Chloe. 'You nearly always do. It's almost like he's yours.' She sighed and looked at her dad. 'I *so* need a pony of my own, Dad.'

Her dad raised his eyebrows. 'You *need* one, do you?'

'Yes. You could get me one for my birthday on Tuesday,' said Chloe hopefully. She ran round to him and knelt down beside him, holding her hands up as if she was praying. 'Please, please, please, please, *please!*'

Her dad leant over and tickled her. She squealed and jumped up.

Erin smiled. She kept asking her dad and stepmum, Jo, for a pony too.

'Come on, you two. Let's get some breakfast inside you,' said Nicky. 'Then we'd better get going. You don't want to be late for your beach ride!'

As soon as they arrived at the stables, they went to the office to find out which ponies they were going to be riding that day. Erin's heart leapt as she saw that she was going to be riding Kestrel, just as she had hoped.

'Yay!' said Chloe happily. 'I've got Misty.' The grey Welsh mountain pony was one of her favourites.

Just then Fran and Katie, two of the other helpers, came in. Erin had once been best friends with them, but they had been really mean ever since they discovered she was going to a different secondary school from them in September.

'We've got Pippin and Tango,' said Katie, checking the board.

Fran snorted. 'No surprise who's got Kestrel, is it?' She swung round, hands on hips. 'You always get to ride him,

Erin. Everyone knows it's just because you're Jackie's little pet!'

Erin swallowed. She hated people being mean to her. Chloe scowled at Fran and opened her mouth to make a sharp retort. But just then the door opened and Jackie, their teacher, came in. 'Hi, girls,' she said cheerfully. 'Have you all seen which ponies you're riding on the beach?'

They nodded, Fran looking as if butter wouldn't melt in her mouth. She was very good at putting on an act around grown-ups.

'Right then, off you go and catch them,' said Jackie. 'We'll head off at eleven.'

The four girls left the office. Kestrel was in a different field from the other

ponies. As Erin reached the gate, she
called his name. He lifted his head from
the grass and whinnied, his ears pricked.
She felt in her pocket for a Polo.
'Come on, boy. Here, Kestrel!'

Kestrel came trotting up the field
towards her. He was a dapple grey
with a long mane, huge dark eyes and
ears that almost seemed to touch at
the tips. He reached her and crunched
the sweet happily while she clipped on
his lead rope. Erin rubbed his forehead.
He reminded her a bit of Tor, but
whereas Tor was a majestic stallion
whom she sometimes felt a bit shy
about patting, Kestrel loved hugs and
cuddles and she never felt shy about
patting him!

She led him back to the yard and

tied him up before she and Chloe set about getting rid of the mud and grass stains on the two ponies' grey coats.

As Erin groomed his shoulder and back, Kestrel turned his head and rested his muzzle on her shoulder.

Jackie walked over. 'He really seems to have taken to you, Erin. I'm a bit worried about how he is settling in at the moment though; he's lost weight since he got here. I'm not sure he's cut out to be a riding-school pony.' She looked thoughtful. 'I've noticed you've been here a lot more in the evenings after school in the last few weeks.'

'Yes, now my SATs are over, my dad says it's fine for me to come down here whenever I'm free,' Erin explained.

'Well, how would you feel about

taking more responsibility for looking after Kestrel – grooming him, feeding him, riding him when you're here? Just for a short while. I wonder if having one regular person who looks after him for a bit might calm him down.'

Erin stared at Jackie, almost too stunned to speak. 'Really? That would be brilliant!'

Jackie smiled. 'Good. I'll speak to your parents and check they're all right with it, but I do think it might help Kestrel to have one carer for a while whom he can bond with.' She sighed. 'If he doesn't settle in soon, I might have to consider selling him.'

'I'm sure he'll be fine. I'll help him settle in better,' said Erin quickly.

'Thank you,' said Jackie, smiling, and she walked away.

Erin swung round to Chloe. 'Can you believe it?' she gasped. 'I'm going to be looking after Kestrel! It'll be almost like he's my very own pony. It'll be just —'

'Yeah. It'll be great for you!' Chloe interrupted abruptly, and walked away.

Erin stared after her. How could she have been so stupid? She'd been so caught up in her own excitement that she'd forgotten to think about Chloe's feelings. She asked herself how she would have felt if it had been the other way round and Jackie had been asking Chloe to look after one of the ponies as if it was her own. She knew immediately that she'd have felt horribly jealous! No wonder Chloe had walked away.

Throwing down her dandy brush, she ran after Chloe. She caught up with her at the field gate. Chloe's back was to her. 'Chloe! I-I'm sorry!' Erin stammered. 'I . . . I'm really sorry,' she

said again helplessly, not knowing what else to say.

Chloe hesitated and then her shoulders sagged. 'Oh, it's OK,' she said, turning round. 'I shouldn't have snapped. Only I'd love it if Jackie asked me to look after a pony.' She took a deep breath and lifted her chin. 'But that's really good, Erin. I'm really pleased for you.'

'So we're still friends then?' asked Erin anxiously.

Chloe grinned, suddenly looking much more like her normal self. 'Best friends! Come on!' she said, linking arms with Erin. 'Let's go and finish grooming.'

Erin walked back up the yard, joy surging through her. She was going to be looking after Kestrel and she had the best friend in the world.

She glanced up and tried to ignore the storm clouds that were beginning to creep across the sky.

Two

After supper that night, Erin went to her bedroom. Downstairs she could hear a car race blaring out on the TV. The rest of her sports-mad family were all in the lounge watching it. She went to her windowsill. There was a wooden box on it that was full of stones with holes in – hagstones. Erin took one out and sat down on her bed with it. She was a special kind of stardust spirit called a weather weaver. Marianne – the dark spirit – was a weather weaver too. Weather weavers could work magic with hagstones and use them for talking to the sky horses. Erin stroked the pale smooth stone in her hand.

There were different types of hagstones and they could all be used to do different kinds of magic. Seeing stones, like the stone in her hand, had a single hole through the centre and they could be used for visions of people and places, and talking to people or sky horses far away. Stones with two holes were called warding stones. They could be used to protect the person holding them from being injured or being watched. There were other stones too, like healing stones, but Erin hadn't learnt how to use those yet.

If Mum was still alive maybe she would have taught me, Erin thought. Her real mum had died almost eight years ago in a car accident. Erin now knew that weather weaving was always inherited, so her mum must have been a weather weaver too.

Erin looked down again at the hagstone in her hands. It was so

strange to think that she had the
power to affect the weather. Tor had
explained to her that weather weavers
worked in harmony with the horses.
Not Marianne though, thought Erin with
a shiver. Marianne wanted to make the
sky horses do whatever she wanted so
that she had complete control over the
weather and everyone would fear her.
Sky horses of royal blood could be
used to control the weather from
Earth, which was why Marianne had
captured Tor.

Erin had used her weather magic to
free him. However, just as Tor had been
about to go back to the skies through
a magic gateway at a place called
World's End, Marianne had tricked his
son, Mistral, into coming through to

look for him. Marianne had imprisoned the foal in a trapping stone and tried to use him to control the weather instead.

Almost two weeks ago, Erin and Chloe had managed to find the trapping stone and Erin had used her powers to break it and free Mistral, but as she had done so the gateway had been destroyed. Now Erin and Chloe were trying to help Mistral and Tor find another gateway so they could return home. *If only we knew where it was*, thought Erin. There was a stardust prophecy that suggested there was another gateway hidden somewhere:

Two gateways now balance the light and the darkness,

One lost in memory, hidden by the sea.
The dark door is reserved for the hand
that creates it.
The other lies close to a whispering tree,
Deep underground and made from
moonlight.
When it is found, then two can be free.

'Lost in memory. Hidden by the sea,'
Erin whispered, thinking hard. 'Deep
underground. Made from moonlight.
Near a whispering tree.'

She frowned. How could something
be underground but hidden by the sea
and be near a tree. It didn't make any
sense. 'What is a whispering tree
anyway?' she wondered. Her fingers
buzzed as if the stone was sending
sparks of electricity into her skin.

Magic, she realized.

She caught her breath as she had
an idea. Could she use the hagstone
to see where the whispering tree
was?

She stared at the hole in the stone
and let her mind go blank apart from
one thought: *the whispering tree.* She let
the words float in and out of her mind,
waiting to see what would happen and
if the hagstone would show her
anything.

Darkness closed in on her and a
picture started to appear inside the hole
in the stone. It grew bigger and bigger
until Erin wasn't sure whether she was
looking at it or whether she was
actually in the vision herself. There was
a tree in front of her. A tall tree with

a gnarled grey trunk and round green leaves with feathered edges hanging down from slender branches. The leaves rustled together in the breeze, making a whispering sound, almost as if they were talking. Erin could hear waves crashing on rocks nearby, but before she could look around and see if she could recognize where she was, the tree started to dissolve and a new vision began to form.

Erin was taken aback. What was happening? Often the visions she had through the stones would fade – Tor had said it was because she wasn't a very experienced weather weaver – but she wasn't used to new visions taking their place. She watched as the picture changed. It was the same tree, but this time there was someone sitting underneath it — a girl wearing wide jeans and a yellow and brown T-shirt and a long coat. She looked about Erin's age and had a fringe and dark hair that curled under at her shoulders. She was writing in a blue

leather diary. She looked up and chewed her pen.

Erin gasped. She knew who it was! She'd seen photos in the photo album downstairs.

Her throat felt dry with shock. 'Mum?' she managed to whisper.

She had a rushing, swirling feeling and then darkness engulfed her. She blinked and found herself back in her room again.

Her heart pounded. *Calm down*, she thought. *It was just a vision.*

But she couldn't calm down. She'd never seen into the past before. And to see her mum when in real life she could hardly remember her . . . Erin couldn't stop trembling.

Her mum had been sitting by the

whispering tree – the very tree Erin
was trying to find – and she had been
writing in a diary . . .

A diary!

Erin's eyes widened as she made the
connection with her real life. Up in the
attic there was a box full of her mum's
old diaries and notebooks. Erin's dad
had said he was keeping them for Erin
when she got older. A few years ago,
Erin had gone through some of them,
but her mum's handwriting had been
quite hard to read and what she'd
deciphered hadn't made much sense. In
the end, she'd given up. She hadn't
thought about the box since then. But
maybe things about stardust and
weather weaving were written in
those diaries and journals! Maybe

there would be a clue about the whispering tree!

Erin jumped to her feet and ran downstairs. The car race was still on. Jo, her dad and her brothers, Jake, Sam and Ben, were all glued to it. 'Dad?' Erin said.

'Later, Erin. It's almost finished.'

'But, Dad, this is important. Can I go into the attic?'

'Why?' asked her dad, not taking his eyes off the telly.

'I just want to look through those old diaries of Mum's.'

That had the effect of getting her dad's attention. He looked swiftly at her. 'Any particular reason, sweetheart?'

'No,' said Erin, shaking her head, seeing Jo glance at her too. 'I just feel like it.'

Her dad frowned. 'OK, well, of course it's fine, but maybe I'll come with you . . .' However, just then there was an excited yell from the commentator on TV, and Erin's brothers and Jo all gasped. 'The Ferrari's gone!' shouted Jake.

Erin's dad's eyes darted back to the TV. Erin quietly left the room. She went back upstairs and up a further flight that led into the attic. It was a long, dark, dusty room and there were boxes and old suitcases everywhere. A single light bulb hung down from the roof. Erin switched it on and a weak yellow light shone out, illuminating the darkness.

Erin spotted the plastic crate very quickly. It was pushed to one side of the attic room. She hurried over and took the lid off. Yes, there were all the diaries! Erin's eyes fell on a blue diary. It looked just like the diary her mum had been writing in when she'd seen her in the vision! She picked it up and looked inside. Her mum had written her name on the first page: *Rachel Margaret Winston, aged 10 and ¾*. It was a two-year diary and there was a lock of dark hair pressed inside the cover, secured with a piece of yellowing sticky tape.

Mum's hair, thought Erin, touching it in awe. It was darker than her own. Gingerly, she turned over the pages of the diary and began to read . . .

CHAPTER
Three

1 January
Well, it's New Year's Day today and the
start of my new diary. My new year's
resolution is to write in my diary every
single day. Even if nothing's happening,
I've decided I'll write about stardust and
weather weaving. Mum has been telling
me loads this Christmas holiday. She says
now I'm nearly eleven I need to know.

The big round hagstone down at World's
End is a gateway between our world and

the cloud world and Mum says that every seven years we have to put a new spell on it so it can't be used by anyone – not sky horse or human. Granny used to do it and now Mum does and I'll have to when I get older. The spell has to be done again on Midsummer's Day next year. It's weird to think that the stone is a gateway and that we could use it to get to the cloud world. I'd love to actually meet a sky horse. Just imagine being able to stroke one. It would be brilliant! But Mum says it's really bad for the horses if the gateways get used too much. They get ill or something. There's another gateway as well as the one at World's End . . .

It was the end of the page. Hardly able to breathe, Erin turned the page over.

This was amazing! Her mum writing about gateways and sky horses! She read on, her eyes struggling to make sense of the scribbled words:

The other gateway's a massive secret. Mum says she thinks only me and her know about it now. Granny created it when she was fighting her sister, May, who was a really dark spirit. I came on my bike today and I'm now sitting by the whispering tree. You'd never ever guess the gateway was close by. I think the whispering tree is the best tree in the whole world. When I sit here, I can almost imagine that it's talking to me. There's a lot of holly here too and at the moment it's got berries all over it. I saw a robin pecking

at the berries a few minutes ago. It was
very sweet . . .

'Erin?'

Erin jumped.

Her dad was standing in the attic
doorway. 'Are you all right, sweetheart?'

'Yes, I'm fine,' said Erin. She'd been
miles away, so excited by what she was
reading in her mum's diary that she'd

almost forgotten she was in the attic.
'Can I take these books to my room,
Dad?'

'Of course,' her dad said. 'I kept them
so that you could read them all one day.
Why the sudden interest though?'

Erin shrugged.

Her dad looked at her. 'Everything is
OK, isn't it? You're not upset by
anything?'

'No, no, everything's fine.' Erin just
wanted to get on and read some more
of the blue diary. 'Can you bring the
box down for me, please, Dad? It's
really heavy.'

Her dad nodded and carried the box
to her bedroom. 'You do know you can
talk to me about your mum at any
time,' he said as he put it on the floor.

'I know,' said Erin. She just wanted to get him out of the room. 'But I'm all right, Dad. Really. I promise.'

'OK then.' Her dad ruffled her hair and left.

Erin sank on to her bed with the blue diary and started to read again.

By bedtime she was up to March in the diary. She hadn't found out any more about where the gateway was, but her mum did write about it one more time. There was an interesting diary entry in February that Erin had read several times:

12 February
Mum and I went for a walk on the cliffs today and she told me more about the

hidden gateway. She said that Granny made it when her sister, May, captured the sky stallion. May was jealous of Granny because everyone said Granny had more power than she did and so May went into the cloud world and captured the sky stallion so that she would have complete control over the weather. She made a great storm happen so that people would be scared of her. It rained for days. Lots of people were killed and places flooded. Granny wanted to make May release the stallion back to the sky. She made the gateway in case she needed to get into the cloud world and couldn't use the gateway at World's End. She didn't need it in the end because she managed to defeat May in a fight, but she must have been a really powerful *weather weaver to have made it. Mum says she thinks Granny and Great-Aunt May were two of the most powerful weather weavers ever. I hope I get to be as powerful as them one day!*

Erin shivered. Tor had told her that there had once been a devastating storm caused by a dark spirit catching a sky stallion. But Erin hadn't realized that the dark spirit had been her great-grandmother's sister, May. *She sounds just like Marianne*, she thought. Horrible images of wild storms, torrential rain and flooding filled her mind. *If Marianne gets control over the weather like Great-Aunt May did*, she realized, *the same thing could happen all over again*.

She was longing to read on and find out more. Maybe there would be other clues as to where the gateway was. As it was, she knew a few more things than she had before she found the diary. It was near holly bushes and near the edge of the cliff and the sea and it was close enough for her mum to cycle to. Surely if she and Chloe flew round the coastal area enough they'd be able to find it?

She shut the diary. She couldn't wait to show Chloe that night!

'Oh wow!' breathed Chloe, when Erin told her.

They had met on the beach, just as they usually did on the days when they weren't staying at each other's houses.

The sea pulled at the shingle beach,
dragging the stones down the beach
with a clatter. There was the smell of
drying seaweed in the air. The full
moon shone down, making Erin's dress
glitter silvery blue. Chloe's dress was
golden. There were four types of
stardust spirit – summer, autumn,
winter and spring. They each wore
different-coloured clothes and could do
different types of magic. Chloe was a
summer spirit, which meant she could
start fires, and Erin, like all weather
weavers, was a winter spirit, which
meant she had the power to make rain,
hail or snow happen around her.

'Does the diary say anything about
the hidden gateway?' Chloe asked.

'Yes!' Erin showed Chloe the first

entry and then turned to the one where her mum had written about the gateway being created.

Chloe's eyes skimmed over it. 'So the dark spirit who captured a sky stallion the time before was your great-grandmother's sister?'

Erin nodded. 'It's weird, isn't it? One sister – my great-granny – must have been good; Great-Aunt May must have been bad.'

Chloe looked thoughtful. 'You know the night you broke the trapping stone, Tor said he thought you and Marianne might be related because your magic exploded with such power when it met. Well, maybe Marianne is May's granddaughter or something like that? Maybe that's how you're related to her.'

Erin considered it. When Tor had
told her what he thought, she had
found it hard to believe him because
as far as she knew she didn't have any
other relatives. Her mum and her
granny had both been only children,
so she didn't have any aunts or cousins,
but now she wondered if Chloe was
right, if the link went back further.
'I'll ask Dad tomorrow if he knows
anything about her.' A shiver ran
through her. She didn't like the
thought of being related to Marianne.
She shut the diary and suddenly
became aware that the back of her
neck was prickling, just like the night
before.

She reached for the warding stone
she usually carried in her pocket. It

would warn her of danger by turning icy cold, but the warding stone wasn't there. Her heart sank. She had been so eager to get out and see Chloe that she'd left the house without it.

She quickly crouched down, moving the stones on the beach with her hands.

Could she find another one? Her skin was still prickling.

'Erin?' said Chloe in surprise. 'What are you doing?'

'Just a minute!' Erin scanned the stones. She'd always had a knack of finding hagstones; other people could look for ages, but she just seemed to spot them straight away. Sure enough she soon discovered a brown stone with two holes and picked it up. Holding it in her hand, she shut her eyes and imagined an invisible shield round her and Chloe, imagined rocks and branches bouncing off it. The stone glowed warm and then cold.

She straightened up and saw that Chloe was staring at her in bafflement.

'Sorry. I had that feeling again, like

Marianne was watching us as we were talking, but I've got a warding stone to protect us now just in case.' Erin glanced around.

Chloe looked worried. 'If she was just watching, she'll have seen the diary.'

Erin's fingers tightened anxiously on the blue book. 'Let's go and meet Tor.'

Chloe nodded. 'We can look for a whispering tree on the way. I brought an old book of Dad's about trees from home.' She pulled a slim leather-bound book out of her pocket. 'I thought we could look through it and see if it gives us any ideas about what type of tree it might be.'

Erin put the diary and the warding stone in her pocket and took the guidebook. 'I saw the tree in a vision today. I think I know what it looks like.' She began to turn over the pages of the book. 'No, not that one. Not that one . . .' She stopped. 'There! That's it!'

She read out the name. 'Aspen.'

Chloe peered over her shoulder and read out. 'The slightest breeze flutters the green leaves of the aspen, hence its folk name – the whispering tree.' She looked at Erin in excitement. 'You're right! It is an aspen tree we have to find. At least we know what we're after now. Come on, but let's camouflage ourselves first.'

All stardust spirits could camouflage themselves, using magic to blend into the background. Erin started to nod, but just then the air behind her flickered. Erin gasped as a woman with long blonde hair appeared. She landed lightly on the shingle, her silvery-blue dress shining in the starlight as she pointed at the girls.

The woman's voice hissed out like a breath of ice in the night. '*Bind them!*'

Four

Erin pulled Chloe down just in time
as Marianne shot a blast of white light
at them.

Chloe reacted instantly, using her
own stardust magic.

'Fire be with me!' she yelled. A
burning fireball burst from her fingers
and flew at Marianne.

Marianne snapped her fingers and a
small icy cloud appeared between her
and the girls. As the fireball shot through

it, the flames extinguished and it
vanished with a crack. Marianne
clenched her fist. The cloud turned into
a ball of ice. She flicked open her fingers
with a laugh. The ball immediately spun
straight towards Chloe's head.

Erin shoved the tree guide in her
pocket with the diary and grabbed the
warding stone. She squeezed it tight.
Protect us. Protect us, she willed it.

The ball of ice seemed to hit a wall
and bounce away. Erin felt a rush of
relief, but she knew her weather magic
wasn't very powerful yet and the
warding stone she had made so hastily
wouldn't be strong enough to protect
them from Marianne for long.

Marianne advanced on them. 'I want
that diary,' she said coldly.

'No,' said Erin, shaking her head and backing up towards the sea. 'You can't have it.'

Marianne's eyes glittered like blue ice. 'Impudent child! Give it to me *now*!' She pointed her hand at Erin's pocket and muttered a word. Erin gasped as she felt the warding stone crack in two!

Marianne swung round and pointed at Chloe. 'Bind her!' she snapped, shooting out white light again.

Chloe didn't move fast enough. She cried out, her voice cutting off abruptly as this time the magic did hit her. Her hands were pinned to her side as if held there by thick rope.

Erin stared at her in dismay. She knew that the only way to break free from a binding spell was if the dark spirit casting it was distracted, but how could she do that? Suddenly she had an idea. She reached into her pocket for the diary.

Marianne took an eager step towards her just as Erin had hoped, Marianne's eyes on her and not on Chloe. 'Hail be with me!' Erin shouted, grabbing her opportunity and pointing at Marianne's head with her other hand. Marianne looked up, properly distracted now as hail started to fall.

Chloe took her chance and broke free of the binding magic, sending a fireball firing straight at Marianne's feet. The dark spirit staggered back in surprise.

'Come on, Erin!' Chloe yelled, vanishing against the dark sky. Erin was just about to camouflage herself when Marianne sprang towards her. Swooping through the air, her body started to change shape, her arms becoming wings, feathers covering her body.

Suddenly where Marianne had been there was now a black-feathered hawk with a curving beak and long talons!

For a moment Erin was too astonished to move. The hawk flew straight at Erin's face. Yelling in shock and alarm, Erin twisted away from the sharp beak. The hawk's talons ripped through Erin's pocket, through the thin fabric of her dress, slashing down Erin's leg. As Erin cried out in pain, the hawk grabbed the book in her cruel beak before flapping her wings and shooting up into the sky. In an instant she had disappeared.

'D-did you see that?' stammered Chloe, appearing in the air again.

'Marianne turned into a bird!' Erin breathed. She looked down at her leg. The jagged scratch was bleeding heavily.

'She got the diary,' said Chloe in dismay.

Erin reached into the remains of her pocket. 'Not quite.' She pulled out the small blue diary.

Chloe stared.

Erin smiled shakily. 'She got your dad's book on trees!'

'Marianne's got the wrong book?' Chloe exclaimed.

Erin nodded.

'Oh cool!' The delight on Chloe's face changed swiftly to alarm and concern. 'We'd better get out of here. She's bound to realize and be back any minute! Come on!' She grabbed Erin's hand and flew up into the sky, camouflaging herself at the same time.

'*Camouflagus*,' Erin whispered, and her body disappeared too, blending into the starry background.

They raced through the air, side by side. 'You were right. Marianne must have been watching us earlier,' hissed Chloe. 'She must have heard us talking about the gateway and wants the diary because she thinks it will help her find out where it is!'

They reached the woods and flew down into the clearing. Tor and Mistral were waiting for them. The young grey colt whinnied in greeting. 'Hi, boy,' said Chloe, stroking his neck.

Tor looked at Erin's face. He seemed to tell instantly that something was wrong. 'What's been happening?' he asked as she went over to him shakily.

'Lots.' She told him about finding the diary and about looking at it on the beach and about Marianne appearing. 'She turned into a bird,' said Erin, looking down at the deep scratch on her leg. The blood had dried now, but it was still sore. She rubbed it. 'She changed into a hawk, Tor. I didn't know stardust spirits could do that.'

Tor nodded. 'Powerful stardust spirits

can turn into animals and birds, but it
is usually only dark spirits who do
because it disrupts the balance of nature.
You must make sure you carry a
warding stone at all times, Erin.'

'I should have brought one with me
this evening,' said Erin. 'I did manage to
find another on the beach, but
Marianne cracked it. If only I'd come
out with one in the first place – it
would have warned me that she was
coming and we could have got away
before she arrived. I can't believe I was
so stupid!' She sighed.

'At least you've still got the diary,'
Chloe reminded her.

Erin nodded. 'My mum wrote lots of
things about weather weaving in it.'

'This could be very important. Keep

it at your house,' advised Tor. 'It is not safe to carry it around. Now Marianne knows about it, I am sure she will come back and try to steal it from you again. You must read it carefully. It may tell us all we need to know.'

Erin looked at him. There was something that had been on her mind ever since she had seen the vision of her mum. 'Tor, how come I saw Mum? I mean, she's . . . she's dead.'

'Visions can be of the past or the present,' replied Tor. 'When you are more practised with your powers, you will be able to use seeing stones to look into the past whenever you want.' He glanced up at the sky; thick clouds were starting to edge across it. 'We cannot talk more

about it now. I need to appear to
my herd.'

If Erin and Tor worked together, Tor
could appear to the horses in the sky
and move among his herd while he was
actually here on Earth. They would
follow him and do as he commanded,
letting him change the weather.

Erin and Chloe set out hagstones in a
circle. Mistral tried to help by rolling
stones to the circle with his nose, but he
always ended up pushing them too far.
Chloe giggled at him and he butted her
with his head. She rubbed his neck and
he snorted happily. Erin smiled. It was
sometimes hard to imagine that one day
he would be as majestic as Tor, but
already she could see it in the way he
held his head, the pride in his eyes, the

curve of his neck. She suddenly realized how lucky she was to be able to get to know and to talk to two sky horses.

Tor stepped into the circle. 'Are you ready, Erin?'

Erin took a deep breath. Trying to clear her mind of Marianne and what had just happened, she nodded slowly. 'Ready.'

She followed Tor into the circle, her heart beating fast at the thought of doing weather-weaving magic again. He touched her shoulder with his nose and their eyes met. Sometimes they didn't need to talk. Sitting down on the ground, she took a seeing stone out of her pocket. She remembered how nervous she had felt the very first time she had tried to work this type of weather magic with Tor just a few weeks ago. She was beginning to get used to it now. The stone felt as if it was trembling in her hand.

Tor snorted softly. Erin stared at the hole in the centre of the seeing stone. The edges of her sight blurred. 'Sky horses, I ask you to come,' she murmured.

Tor seemed to blur, dissolving from flesh and bone into silvery mist. The mist spiralled round and re-formed. Tor appeared again, the size of a model horse, his body almost see-through, his mane and tail glittering like snow crystals. Around the edge of the circle of stones other sky horses, all a similar size, started to appear. Some had their heads down grazing, others were playing

or rolling. Erin watched them, knowing
that it was an exact picture of what was
happening in the clouds above them.

A beautiful white mare with a
sweeping mane and tail cantered up to
Tor. *Snowdance*, thought Erin, *Tor's lead
mare*. Over the last few weeks she had
got to know the horses, and she knew
how fond Tor and Snowdance were of
each other. Snowdance looked very
relieved to see Tor. She stopped in
front of him and they touched noses,
their eyes half closing.

But they could not stand still for
long. On the outskirts of the herd, there
was a group of mares with foals who
were pacing around anxiously, and a
young stallion called Lightning and his
friends were fighting. Erin watched as

Tor trotted over to the mares. He
moved proudly, his ears pricked, his tail
floating like a banner. The agitated
mares crowded round him. He moved
among them, touching noses, breathing
gently muzzle to muzzle. Slowly the
tension left the horses and they began
to look calmer.

Meanwhile Snowdance went over to
the young stallions. The fighting that
had started playfully was becoming
more serious. Lightning landed a kick
on one of the other colts' side and
grazed his teeth down another colt's
shoulder. As Snowdance came over, he
put his ears back and squealed at her
as if daring her to stop him. She
approached him, her own ears
flattened. He turned round and kicked

out with his back legs. Looking angry, she dodged his hooves and nipped him sharply on the back before closing in to bite the crest of his neck.

Lightning began to canter away and then seemed to think again. He stopped and confronted the mare. Tor came galloping over. Lightning shot off. Tor chased after him, driving him on. The younger stallion soon began to tire. He lowered his head as if offering an apology. Tor stopped and let him slow to a walk. Lightning turned and looked at him. There was a long pause and then Tor snorted and Lightning walked slowly over. Tor turned haughtily and walked back to the herd with Lightning following him.

Erin could have sat watching the sky

horses all night, but Tor began to lead
them across the stone circle. They
followed him obediently. Tor led them
all the way to the stones at the edge of
the circle. There he stopped, but the
other horses carried on walking and
disappeared.

Erin knew that if she looked up she
would see the clouds above her
disappearing over the horizon. When
the circle inside the stones was clear,
Tor looked at her and whinnied and
Erin's fingers closed over the hole in
the stone. 'End,' she whispered.

Darkness fell over her eyes. As it
cleared, she blinked. Tor was standing in
front of her, back to his normal size, his
body solid again.

'Snowdance is so beautiful,' said Erin.

'She misses me and Mistral very much,' replied Tor heavily. 'At least the skies are quiet again now,' he said, glancing up. 'But the unrest grows every day. Brief visits from me cannot keep the skies properly calm for long, the herd need a leader with them full time. Lightning is young but ambitious. His strength is growing. Snowdance will always stay loyal to me, and many others will follow her lead, but if I do not return, violent fights will break out among the herd and that will bring great storms to the coast. I must go home as soon as possible for the sake of my herd and the sake of people living here.'

'We'll find the gateway and get you back,' said Chloe, from outside the circle. 'We've found out what type of tree the whispering tree is and there are some clues in Erin's mum's diary about it. It's near a cliff and it's got holly bushes around it. We're going to go and look for it.'

'I hope you find it,' said Tor worriedly.

'We'll try,' Erin promised him.

★

But although she and Chloe flew around for several hours and saw all sorts of trees, even a few aspen trees, they couldn't find an aspen tree growing in a place like the vision Erin had had and eventually they gave up for the night.

When Erin got home, she flew in through her window and landed on her bedroom floor. 'Stardust be gone,' she whispered. A heaviness sank over her as she became her normal self again, her stardust dress turning into pyjamas. Stretching, Erin got into bed. She tucked the diary under her pillow. Tomorrow she would read some more.

Erin woke up early the next morning. When she went downstairs, she found her dad in the kitchen, washing up from the night before. 'Morning,' he said.

'Hi.' Erin sat down, grateful for the peace and quiet.

'Sleep well?' her dad asked as he put a pan on the draining board.

'Mmmm.' Erin hesitated, remembering what she'd been going to ask him. 'Dad?'

'Yes,' he said, reaching for a towel.

'Do you know anything about my great-grandmother – Mum's granny. She was called Margaret.'

'Yes, I met her quite a few times before she died,' her dad said. 'Why?'

'Oh, Mum just mentions her in her diary,' said Erin. 'Did . . . did you ever meet May, her sister?'

'No. I remember your mum saying

May was the black sheep of the family.
Apparently there was some big
argument with Margaret when she was
younger and after that she left the area.
They never saw each other or spoke
ever again. Your mum tried to trace her
at one point, but her letters were
returned unanswered. May must be
dead now.'

'Did she have any children?' asked
Erin eagerly.

Her dad shook his head. 'No.' He put
the tea towel down and came over. 'Are
you sure there isn't something on your
mind at the moment, love? First
wanting to see your mum's diaries and
now all these questions . . .'

'It's nothing, Dad.' Erin changed the
subject. 'Can I have some toast, please?'

Her dad hesitated and then shrugged. 'Sure,' he said. 'White bread or brown?'

'Have you read any more of the diary?' whispered Chloe, when she and Erin met in the car park at the stables after school.

'Not yet,' said Erin. 'But I've got it with me. I thought it would be safe to have it here and we can look at it later.'

'Great,' said Chloe. 'Maybe we can find some more clues about where the gateway is.'

Erin nodded. 'I hope so.' She glanced at the yard. 'Let's go and see what Jackie wants us to do today.'

'I'm sure she'll want *you* to catch *your* pony,' Chloe teased her. 'And groom *your* pony and ride *your* pony. Are you sure you'll have enough time to think about any of the other ponies?'

Erin punched her arm.

They set off towards the yard but just then a silver Land Rover with a new trailer attached drove into the car park. Inside the trailer, a horse whinnied.

'Smart trailer,' commented Chloe. 'It must be someone coming for a lesson . . .' She broke off as the Land Rover stopped, the driver's door opened and someone stepped out. Erin gasped.

It was Marianne!

CHAPTER

Five

Erin felt frozen to the spot. Marianne
had been to the stable once before,
but that was before they had known
she was a dark spirit. Now she
surveyed the car park. She was
wearing black breeches and riding
boots and a plain white fitted T-shirt.
Her blonde hair was tied back in a
neat knot at the base of her neck. She
looked very elegant, but completely
ordinary.

Chloe grabbed Erin's hand. 'Quick! Run!' she said in panic.

They both ran up the yard. Erin glanced round and saw a cold, amused smile on Marianne's face as she watched them.

When the girls reached the top of the yard by the back stable block, they stopped, panting. 'What's she doing here?' Chloe demanded.

'She does know Jackie,' Erin reminded her.

'She's up to something,' Chloe groaned. 'I wish we could talk to Tor.'

'We can,' Erin said, her fingers touching a long white hair that was wound carefully round her watchstrap. 'I've still got the hair from his mane. I keep it with me all the time. I can use it to talk to him if I need to.'

'Brilliant!' said Chloe. 'Ask him what we should do!'

Erin checked there was no one around and closed her fingers on the hair. *Tor,* she thought. *Tor, I need you.*

'What is it?' Tor replied immediately.

She felt a rush of relief as she heard his strong, warm voice.

'Chloe and I are at the stables and Marianne's here. What shall we do?'

'Marianne is with you?'

Erin heard the alarm in his voice. 'Yes.'

There was a pause. 'Do nothing,' he said at last. 'She will not attempt to hurt you with so many other people around.'

'But . . .' Erin began.

'There is nothing you can do. You
cannot tell anyone about her true
nature. They would not believe you.
She will not harm you, I am sure,
but stay close to other people just in
case.'

'OK,' said Erin, her heart starting to
slow down.

'I will see you tonight,' said Tor
reassuringly.

'Yes, tonight,' replied Erin. Letting go
of the hair, she looked at Chloe.

'What did he say?' demanded Chloe.

'He doesn't think she is after us.' Erin
repeated what Tor had said. 'I guess we
just keep out of her way.'

'Suits me. I like the bit about
sticking near to other people too!' said
Chloe.

They walked cautiously back down
the yard and stopped as they reached
the tack room. Marianne was walking
towards Jackie's office, talking to Fran.
Hanging back where she couldn't see
them, they watched as she went inside.

Fran came over to the tack room.

'Who . . . who was that woman?'

asked Chloe innocently, stepping
forward. Erin heard a faint shake in
her voice, but Fran didn't notice
anything odd.

'Oh, just a friend of Jackie's. She's
going to be keeping her two horses at
livery here for a few months because she's
too busy to look after them at home.'

Erin swallowed. That could mean
Marianne coming down every day to
the stables!

'I bet her horses are lovely,' Fran
went on obliviously. 'Did you see her
trailer? It's brand new.'

Just then Jackie came out of the
office with Marianne. They were
chatting and smiling. 'These three are
some of my pony helpers,' Jackie said.
'You'll probably see quite a bit of them

when you're here, Marianne. This is Fran and Erin and Chloe.'

Marianne looked at Chloe and Erin and her mouth curved into a smile. 'I've met you before, haven't I?' she said as if she didn't really know them. 'I hope you'll be able to help show me around a bit.'

'Of course we will!' said Fran eagerly. Neither Erin nor Chloe said a word. Erin's skin felt like it was prickling all over. She shrank back.

'The stables are this way,' said Jackie cheerfully to Marianne. 'I'll take you around and then give you a hand unloading the horses.'

'Thank you,' said Marianne brightly. 'See you later, girls.' And with that she followed Jackie across the yard.

★

Jackie helped Marianne unload her horses, two sleek thoroughbreds — a dark bay called Gemini and a chestnut called Gamble.

'What are we going to do?' whispered Erin to Chloe as they groomed Kestrel and Pippin. 'She's going to be here all the time now!' She usually really loved going to the stables, but if Marianne was down on the yard too it would be awful. Marianne might be unlikely to hurt them in the daylight, but they weren't going to be able to relax for a second. Erin put her arms round Kestrel's neck and hugged him. He nuzzled her affectionately.

'So what are these two ponies' names then?' Marianne's voice cut through the air.

Erin jumped in fright, making Kestrel startle and pull back sharply on his lead rope, breaking the bale string he was tied to.

'Steady, boy,' said Erin quickly, grabbing him before he could escape.

'The Arab pony is Kestrel and Chloe

is grooming Pippin,' said Jackie, who
had led Marianne across to where the
girls stood with the ponies.

'He looks a bit flighty,' commented
Marianne, nodding at Kestrel as Erin
retied him to another bit of bale string.

'He is a bit, but he's fairly new and
Erin's helping me try to settle him in,'
Jackie explained.

'Hmm,' said Marianne, frowning as
Kestrel began pawing at the concrete
with a front hoof, getting increasingly
agitated as he picked up on Erin's
tension. 'I wouldn't say he looks ideal
for a riding-school pony, Jackie.'

Jackie looked rather worriedly at
Kestrel, who was still pawing the
ground, and then they walked off.

Erin groaned. The last thing she

wanted was Jackie wondering if
Kestrel was cut out to be in a riding
school. 'Oh, Kestrel. Why did you have
to play up so much when they were
watching?'

'I can't believe Marianne said that,'
said Chloe angrily.

Remembering how Tor had calmed
the mares the night before by nuzzling
their necks, Erin lightly stroked
Kestrel's neck, shoulder and mane,
talking to him softly all the time.
Gradually Kestrel stopped scraping the
ground and began to relax, his
expression softening. Erin breathed
gently into his nostrils. He breathed in
and then blew out; the rest of the
tension seemed to leave his body.

Erin rested her forehead against his

neck. She knew that Jackie was already worried about him; the last thing she needed was Marianne stirring up trouble.

'It'll be OK,' said Chloe softly, looking at her from the other side of Pippin.

Erin really hoped she was right.

CHAPTER

Six

By the time Erin got home, she was
more determined than ever that she
and Chloe had to get Tor and Mistral
back to the sky as soon as possible.
Maybe once that was done Marianne
would leave them alone.

*We have to find the gateway before she
does*, Erin thought as she settled down
on her bed and picked up her mum's
diary. She was up to the month of June
now. She read through the first couple

of weeks. There was nothing of particular interest, just her mum talking about school and the stables she went riding at. It was fun to read, but it didn't give Erin any more clues about the gateway. However, when she got to the third week of June, she stiffened.

21 June
Today is the longest day of the year. This time next year Mum will have do the spell on the gateway at World's End to keep it sealed for another seven years. She's going to let me help and the time after that I'll be doing it all by myself. Mum says we need to get a silver bowl and a grey feather and then we take them to the gateway at midnight and do magic. I can't wait until next year to find out

exactly what we have to do! She took me down to the hidden gateway tonight. I've only ever seen it from above by the whispering tree. It was very strange to get to it from the other side. We had to wait for ages until the tide was out enough before we could see the entrance. It smelt of seaweed and was wet and very dark inside, but Mum had put some candles in the cave and she had some matches with her. I didn't like it. I kept imagining someone pushing a boulder across the entrance and shutting us in. We got through the cave and the tunnel and found the gateway. It was amazing! You'd never ever know from above. Sitting by the tree, it just looks like a hole, of course. Mum says that's why it's called the hidden gateway. I was very glad when we got *back outside though! Mum's calling — I'd better go now!*

Erin skimmed over the next few entries, but there was nothing else about the gateway. She looked back over the entry. So the hidden gateway was reached from the seashore by the sound of it: *We had to wait for ages until the tide was out before we could see the entrance*, her mum had written.

So you can see the gateway if you're sitting by the whispering tree, she puzzled. *But you get to it from the bottom of the cliffs.*

She looked out of the window in frustration. It was still light outside. She wanted to get out and start looking straight away . . .

★

Before Erin and Chloe could start searching for the gateway that night, Erin helped Tor calm the sky horses again. 'It's amazing watching the horses in the stone circle, isn't it?' said Chloe when they flew off afterwards to find the gateway.

Erin nodded. It *was* amazing. She sometimes imagined what it would be like to actually go into the clouds and see the sky horses for real, but she remembered what her mum had said in her first diary entry: *it's really bad for the horses if the gateways get used too much.*

'I'll really miss Tor and Mistral when they go back and we can't see them any more,' said Chloe.

'First we've got to get them back,' Erin reminded her. She checked the warding stone in her pocket. It was cool to touch, but not icy. There was no obvious danger.

'Why don't we fly along the beach to see if we can find anything that looks like it might be an entrance?' said Chloe.

Erin nodded. 'OK.'

However, when they reached the sea, their plan was dashed. The tide was in, swelling over the shingle and hiding the first few metres at the base of the cliffs.

'Oh,' said Chloe in disappointment.

'We should have checked when the tide was going to be out,' said Erin.

'Never mind.' Chloe looked around. 'We can still keep looking for a whispering tree; we know now it's got to be at the top of the cliffs.'

They flew over the cliff top, but didn't find any aspen trees surrounded by holly. They did find a young hedgehog that had got stuck in an old plastic cup someone had thrown away though. They freed it and watched it disappear thankfully into the

undergrowth. Then they scared a fat tabby cat away from a woodlark's nest and cleared up a load of old fishing line that had become tangled around some trees. It felt strange to Erin to be doing normal stardust things – helping nature in little ways – when she knew there was something so much bigger they should be doing. *But*, she reminded herself, *all these things are important to the birds and animals we're helping*.

Finally she and Chloe gave up looking for the night. 'I'll ask Dad if he knows when low tide is tomorrow,' said Erin. 'And if it's when we're out here we can look at the cliffs then. Oh, and happy birthday!' she added with a smile. 'It's past midnight so it's already your birthday. Are you coming to the stables tomorrow after school? I can give you your present then.'

Chloe nodded. 'I thought Mum would say I had to do something boring like inviting people round for tea, but she hasn't this year. She said I can go to the stables.'

'Cool!' said Erin. 'I'll see you there then.'

'I wonder what Mum and Dad will get me,' sighed Chloe. 'I hope it's a pony.'

Erin grinned. 'Dream on!'

As soon as Erin got back from school the next day, she changed into her riding gear, put Chloe's birthday present – a silver pendant with a rearing horse on it – into her backpack and cycled

down to the stables. Her heart sank
when she saw Marianne's silver Land
Rover in the car park.

'Hi, Erin,' said Jackie, coming out of
the tack room with a coffee as Erin
went on to the yard. 'Are Chloe and
her parents here yet?'

'No, I don't think so.' Erin felt a bit
surprised. Why had Jackie asked if
Chloe's parents were there? 'What
would you like me to do? Shall I bring
Kestrel in?'

'Yes, please,' replied Jackie.

Erin fetched Kestrel's lead rope and
headed down the yard towards the
fields. On the way she noticed a new
chestnut pony looking over one of the
stable doors.

'Hello,' Erin said, stopping to stroke

him. He was about thirteen hands high
and had a white blaze and a short
sticking-up mane. Looking over the
door, Erin saw that he had two white
socks. He seemed very friendly. 'I
wonder what you're called,' she said.
She looked around, but Jackie had
gone. She wondered if he was a new
riding-school pony or a new livery.
Giving him a last pat, she hurried
down the field to get Kestrel.

The grey pony whinnied and came
trotting up the field to meet her. 'Oi!'
She grinned as he rubbed his head
against her so hard that he almost
knocked her over. Erin noticed that
Marianne's two thoroughbreds were
turned out with him, both with smart
maroon-coloured New Zealand rugs on.

As she turned to walk Kestrel back
to the gate, she gasped in fright.
Marianne was standing by the gate,
staring at her.

Erin's heart thudded as she looked at
the black-clad figure watching her.
There was only one gate in the field
and she was going to have to walk past
Marianne to get through it. Kestrel
tossed his head uneasily. 'Steady, boy,'
said Erin quickly, but her voice shook
and Kestrel began sidestepping and
pulling back.

Marianne came through the gate and
started walking towards Erin.

Erin was occupied with trying to
calm Kestrel and, almost before she
knew what was happening, Marianne
had reached her and taken hold of

Kestrel's head collar. Before Erin could stop her, she'd put a hand between Kestrel's eyes and muttered something.

Kestrel immediately stood still. He stared at the dark spirit. Marianne whispered something to him and all the tension seemed to leave his eyes. He stood, his eyes almost vacant, as if he was in a trance.

'What have you done to him?' demanded Erin, her voice high.

'Nothing.' Marianne smiled coldly. 'Just calmed him down.'

She put a hand on Kestrel's neck. He didn't move a muscle. 'He looks very quiet now, doesn't he?' she said, almost musingly. 'But he really isn't cut out to be a riding-school pony. You know, maybe I should suggest to Jackie that I buy him and take him off her hands.'

'No!' The word burst fiercely out of Erin.

Marianne's blue eyes glinted. 'Well, of course, I could always reconsider if a certain diary found its way into my hands . . .'

Erin stared at her. So she had to give

Marianne the diary or Marianne would buy Kestrel!

Marianne looked icily at her. 'The choice is yours, Erin. Which is it to be?'

CHAPTER
Seven

'Erin!'

Erin looked at the gate. Chloe was scrambling over it, her face alarmed as she stared at Marianne. Erin could see Chloe's parents standing chatting with Jackie near the stables.

Marianne's gaze barely flickered from her face. 'Give me the diary, Erin,' she said. 'Do not make things harder for yourself, because, I promise you, I *will* get it. Even if you choose it above keeping Kestrel, I have seen the address book in Jackie's office now. I know where you and your family live . . .'

Her words seemed to hang in the air.

Chloe came racing across the grass. 'Leave Erin alone!' she cried bravely.

Marianne looked round. 'Hello, Chloe. How nice to see you.' She smiled broadly, but the smile did not reach her eyes. 'I was just giving Erin a hand bringing Kestrel in. He was being a bit troublesome, but he seems fine now. For the time being, at least.' She turned and walked back towards the gate. Erin saw her click her fingers behind her back. Instantly Kestrel started as if he had suddenly come out of a daze. His head shot up and he snorted in alarm.

'Are you OK?' demanded Chloe,
looking at Erin.

Erin nodded, her attention
momentarily focused on Kestrel,
calming him with strokes and pats. 'Yes,'
she gasped, and Chloe looked relieved.
'But Marianne said —'

Chloe interrupted. 'Listen, if you're
OK, I don't want to think about her

for a moment. I don't want her spoiling my news.'

Erin frowned. 'What news?'

'You'll never guess!' Chloe's face broke into the broadest grin possible. 'Oh, Erin! Mum and Dad have bought me a pony for my birthday!'

'What?' Erin whispered.

'I know! I couldn't believe it! They drove me here and they said my birthday present was waiting on the yard. I began to wonder and then I saw Jackie and she pointed to one of the stables. There was a new pony in there, a chestnut . . .'

'I know. I saw him,' said Erin, jealousy shooting through her.

'He's called Ziggy.' Excitement bubbled out of Chloe. 'He's gorgeous and he's mine! Oh, Erin, I can't believe it. I've got a pony of my very own!'

It gradually seemed to dawn on Chloe that Erin wasn't leaping about with joy. 'You . . . you are OK about it, aren't you?' she said.

Kestrel pushed his head against Erin's arm. She remembered what a good friend Chloe had been when Jackie had asked her to look after him. *There's too much else going on for us to fall out*, she realized. She forced herself to smile. 'Sorry. I *am* pleased for you, Chloe. I really am.'

Relief flooded Chloe's face. 'Phew! You can help me look after Ziggy and ride him and when I go away you can look after him for me. He'll be like your pony too then. We can ride him and Kestrel together.'

'If Kestrel's still here,' Erin muttered.

'What?' Chloe frowned.

But Erin didn't want to spoil Chloe's happiness. 'Oh, nothing. It's just something that Marianne said, but I'll tell you later. It's not important,' she lied.

'Really?' Chloe questioned.

Erin nodded. 'Really. Come on, I want to meet Ziggy properly.'

Chloe smiled at her. 'Cool!' And together they led Kestrel up the field.

Ziggy was lovely. Jackie had helped choose him for Chloe and she gave Chloe a lesson on him once Chloe had tacked him up. Erin sat on the fence and watched. At first, Chloe looked a bit nervous to be riding her very own pony, but Ziggy was very well behaved. He was lively and keen to go, but not too excitable or jumpy. Chloe walked, trotted and cantered him and then did a couple of jumps.

'Well done!' praised Jackie as Chloe slowed him down after the second jump. 'I think you two are going to be very well suited.'

Chloe halted Ziggy and looked at Erin. 'Can Erin have a go?'

'Of course!' Jackie smiled. 'You don't have to ask me. He's your pony, Chloe.'

'Hey, Erin!' Chloe called, dismounting. 'Why don't you ride him now?'

As Erin mounted, her jealousy from earlier faded. It was going to be brilliant that Chloe had a pony. They'd be able to do all sorts of fun things together. They could ride Kestrel and Ziggy together in the school, they could groom and clean tack together. It would be great!

But, even as she thought that, she caught sight of Marianne watching from the stable block and her stomach turned over. They could do all those things

provided Marianne didn't carry out her
threat of buying Kestrel.

Ziggy tossed his head as if sensing
that her thoughts were elsewhere. Erin
forced herself to focus on riding. She
would have to decide what to do about
Marianne later. *But what can I do?* she
thought.

She hoped she might get a chance to

talk to Chloe when they had finished riding, but Chloe's mum and dad had brought a cake down to the stables and there was no chance for the two girls to talk on their own.

Tonight, Erin thought. *We can talk then.*

★

★　★

CHAPTER

Eight

'I believe in stardust. I believe in stardust. I believe in stardust,' Erin whispered later that evening.

On the last word, all the heaviness seemed to drain from her body. She swirled round, her pyjamas changing into her stardust dress. Feeling feather-light, she rose into the air. She looked at the diary that was lying beside her bed.

I know where you and your family live.

Marianne's words echoed through her brain. What had the dark spirit meant by that? Had she meant she would come to Erin's house to get the diary? Or that she would maybe hurt her family? Erin glanced uneasily through the window at the dark night. Maybe Marianne was waiting out there for her to go, and then she would come into her room. Erin couldn't shut the window because then she wouldn't be able to get back in. She hesitated. Should she leave the diary as Tor had told her to the other night?

No.

She picked it up and slipped it into her pocket along with a seeing stone and a warding stone. She immediately felt better knowing it was with her. *I'll camouflage myself*, she decided. *Even if Marianne is watching, she won't see me.*

She set off through the window. She was longing to see Chloe and tell her what Marianne had said. Then maybe they could decide what to do. Also, her dad had told her that low tide was at

eleven thirty that night. They had to make the most of the sea being out and get looking for the gateway!

To Erin's relief, Chloe was already waiting on the beach for her. The tide was right out and the shingle beach showed a bigger expanse of stones than normal. The moon was a silver disc in the sky.

'So what was going on with you and Marianne today?' demanded Chloe as Erin landed and let her camouflage fade. 'What was she saying?'

'She wants the diary.' Erin quickly told her what Marianne had said about buying Kestrel and about knowing where she lived. 'I can't let her buy Kestrel!'

'Of course you can't,' said Chloe, horrified.

'But I can't give her the diary either. Oh, Chloe, what do you think she meant by saying she knows where I live? Do you think she meant she would go to my house and steal the diary, or maybe . . . maybe that she would do something to my family?' Erin felt tears start in her eyes. She'd been worrying about it ever since she had seen Marianne that afternoon. 'I don't know what to do.'

Chloe squeezed her hand. 'It's OK. We'll find the entrance that leads to the gateway, set Tor and Mistral free, seal the gateway like your mum talks about and then Marianne can't do anything, even if she does get the diary!'

Seeing the determination in Chloe's eyes, Erin felt a little bit better.

'Come on, let's start looking right away!' said Chloe.

They flew over the beach, their eyes scanning the cliffs to the side of them. 'How about we go round the headland,'

said Chloe. 'We haven't looked on the other side yet.'

'OK,' agreed Erin. They flew on, past the rocks at World's End, two tall stones like fingers pointing at the sky and the blasted remains of the giant hagstone that had once been big enough for adults to climb through. It was now broken into pieces that lay on the rocky spit of land. Erin had heard her dad saying that people thought it must have been hit by lightning, but she and Chloe knew the truth. It had been hit by powerful magic – her magic and Marianne's. As Erin thought of the moment when the magic had hit and the stone had exploded, she shuddered. It had been really scary. Marianne could have injured them, done anything to them, if her magic hadn't collided with Erin's and hit the stone.

They were flying on the other side of the headland now. They didn't usually go round to that side of the headland because the sea was wilder and the winds stronger. The coastline looked different too. When the sea was in, it came right up to the bottom of the cliffs so there was no beach, just rocks. The cliffs were steeper, with bare expanses of soil and gravel, broken only by tufts of long grass and pale tree roots sticking out. There were trees along the tops of the cliffs.

Chloe frowned. 'The aspen tree could be one of those trees.'

'Mmm.' Erin was feeling strange. Her skin was prickling. She reached for the warding stone she had put in her pocket earlier. It felt icy cold. Her heart flipped with fear. 'Chloe! I think Marianne might be watching us. The warding stone is really cold. Let's camouflage our –'

But before she could say anything else there was a savage, shrieking scream. Both girls jumped as a large, black-feathered hawk appeared out of nowhere and dived straight towards Erin, cruel beak open.

Erin dodged just in time, the stone cracking in her hands as the hawk flew straight at her. '*Camouflagus!*' she gasped as the hawk's beak slashed at the air just where she had been hovering.

She saw Chloe disappear at the same time. They had to get away! Hoping

that Chloe would be thinking the same,
Erin began to fly upwards so that she
could fly over the hawk and across the
cliff top, but as she did so she saw
the hawk change back into Marianne.

The dark spirit turned, her back
to the cliff, knowing they were there
in the darkness. Raising her hands she
pointed to the sky. 'Rain be with me!'
she commanded.

Rain began to pour down out of
the sky – not just light rain like Erin
could conjure, but falling in a deluge.
Erin gasped and struggled to keep her
camouflage up as it poured over her
head. She looked at Marianne and saw
that she had somehow managed to cast
a magic barrier around herself so that
the rain fell around her but not a

single drop fell on her. Water streamed over Erin's hair and down her body. She dashed it from her eyes, just in time to see Marianne raise her hands again.

'Hail be with me!' Erin heard Marianne snap out and suddenly the rain changed to hailstones, balls of ice as big as marbles.

Erin cried out as they battered against her. It felt as if someone was pelting her with stones. Putting up her hands to shield her face, she tried to fly upwards, but it was impossible. The hail was forcing her down towards the jagged rocks. She couldn't see anything. Where was Chloe? How close was she to the rocks below?

Erin knew she had lost her

camouflage, but that was the least of her worries. The hailstones beat against her, driving her lower and lower.

Tor, she thought desperately, her hand reaching for the hair round her watch. *Tor, help us!*

CHAPTER

Nine

'Cease!' Marianne hissed.

The hail vanished. Erin looked around, panting. The sky was dark and clear, still again, lit by the full moon. She saw Chloe beneath her, very close to the sharp rocks at the bottom of the cliff, gasping for breath. A minute later and Chloe would have been driven straight into them. Marianne's eyes glittered as she held out her hand. 'I want the diary, Erin. I know you have it with you. I was watching from the darkness and I saw you put it into your pocket. Give it to me.'

'No,' said Erin, shaking her head.

Marianne pointed at the skies again. 'Hail be with me!' she snapped.

The hail started again. Erin heard Chloe scream.

'Stop it!' yelled Erin, fear for Chloe

exploding through her. 'Stop it! You can have the diary!'

The hail ceased.

Marianne looked at Erin triumphantly. 'I thought you'd see sense.'

Erin gave Chloe a desperate look.

Chloe glanced at the cliff and then gasped, 'Give it to her!'

Erin felt a flicker of surprise. She'd thought that Chloe would try to persuade her not to. She hesitated.

Marianne raised her hands again.

'Do it, Erin!' Chloe urged.

Erin made up her mind, grabbed the diary and thrust it into Marianne's hands. If Marianne conjured more hail, Chloe would be driven on to the rocks and injured badly. She couldn't let that happen.

Marianne raced upwards as Chloe started to fly towards Erin. 'Now, I cannot be stopped!' the dark spirit cried. 'I will control the skies!'

'We'll stop you!' Chloe shouted fiercely.

'Really?' said Marianne. 'Hail be with me! Fog be with me!' The words snapped out and the next moment the hail started to fall again, but it was worse this time because a thick mist swirled around them too.

Erin could see nothing but white, could feel nothing but hailstones battering into her body. She didn't know where she was flying. She was lost in a white world, unable to see anything. 'Chloe!' she shouted, reaching out desperately. 'Chloe! Where are you?'

'I'm near the cliff! Help!'

Erin dived down as best she could, her hand reaching out blindly as she tried to work out where Chloe was. Her fingertips touched Chloe's. Chloe grasped on. The hailstones battered down at them. They tried to fly upwards, but the battering of the frozen ice was too strong. They were both forced downwards.

'We're going to hit the rocks!' yelled Erin, holding on tight to Chloe's hands. She tensed her body, waiting to crash into the rocks.

But as she did so she felt a warmth swirl around her, the feel of a horse's mane, a smooth shoulder, breath on her hair.

'Tor?' gasped Erin.

'Hold on to me,' said Tor's voice calmly. Erin grasped blindly at the air around her. Her hands found Tor's neck, his long mane. He was not solid, like a real horse. He was in his cloud form. She could feel him, but at the same time her hands seemed to sink through him as if they were pressing on freshly fallen snow. 'Chloe, hold on to Mistral!' said Tor. 'He is beside you. See us in your heads and you will be able to feel us more solidly beside you.'

Erin imagined Tor, seeing his proud head, his arched neck, his broad back. Her arms wrapped round his neck and she felt him suddenly solid beneath her.

His mane flowed around her. She felt him begin to gallop upwards and was aware of Mistral and Chloe to her right. The two cloud horses swept them out of the mist and landed on the cliff top by some trees. The hail was still falling, but less hard, and the mist that was swirling over where they had been looked like it was starting to clear.

'Can you get rid of the hail and rain now you are safe, Erin?' Tor asked.

'With Marianne gone, the magic will be weakening.'

Erin pointed a hand at the mist and hail and felt stardust magic tingle through her. 'Hail be gone! Mist be gone!'

Gradually the hail stopped and the mist cleared.

Chloe breathed out. 'That was horrible! I thought we were going to die.'

Tor pawed the ground. 'Luckily Erin called to me, and Mistral and I managed to get here in time.'

The colt snorted and rubbed his head against Chloe. 'I'm OK,' Chloe told Mistral. 'Thank you for rescuing me.' She hugged him impulsively.

'And thanks for rescuing me,' Erin

said to Tor. She didn't quite dare to hug him as Chloe had, but she stroked his neck. Since they had landed, he and Mistral had turned back into the usual real-horse forms and he felt reassuringly solid.

'What's been happening?' Tor demanded.

Erin felt sick as the memories came flooding back. 'It's awful, Tor. Marianne's got the diary.'

Tor snorted in alarm. 'What?'

'I'm really sorry. I had to give it to her,' said Erin. She looked at Chloe for back-up, but Chloe had left Mistral and was looking around curiously at the trees. 'I thought she was going to hurt Chloe on the rocks.' Erin's eyes filled with tears as she realized how much she had let Tor down. 'I didn't want to give it to her.' She loyally didn't mention that Chloe had told her to. 'Now she's got it, she'll find the clues to where the gateway is and if she finds it before us she'll use it to get control of the skies before you can get back there and stop her and there'll be storms and floods and everything.'

To her surprise, Tor nuzzled her. 'Erin, you did what you had to.'

'And it doesn't matter anyway,' said Chloe, swinging round from investigating the bushes around them. 'She's not going to find it before us.' They all looked at her. Her eyes shone. 'Because I think we've just found the gateway ourselves!'

CHAPTER

Ten

Erin frowned. 'What do you mean?'

'Look!' Chloe swept her arm around.
'These are holly bushes! And there's an
aspen!' She pointed to a tree near the
edge of the cliff. It had a thick grey
trunk, and leaves that seemed to tremble
and rustle in the breeze. Erin had been
so busy talking to Tor that she hadn't
noticed. Thick bramble bushes clustered
round its base, but the vision of her
mum sitting writing in her diary flashed

into Erin's mind. If the brambles
weren't there . . .

She looked around. This could be just
the place she had seen her mum in the
vision!

'Yes, this could be the right tree,' she
said.

'It's not *just* the tree that makes me
think this is the place where the
gateway might be,' Chloe went on.
'When Marianne had almost driven me
on to the rocks, I saw a cave in the cliff
below. It's hidden from above by a ledge
and the sea would hide it when the
tide is in. I saw it and wondered if it
could be what we were looking for.
That's why I said to give Marianne the
diary. I thought if she had it she'd leave
us alone and we could look around.

Hopefully she's gone back to her house and is reading through it to try and find where the gateway is so we've got some time.'

'Oh, clever stardust spirit,' Tor said. Chloe looked delighted. He stepped forward and nuzzled her cheek.

'You were amazing to notice the cave, Chloe!' said Erin. 'I couldn't think about anything but the rocks.'

'I was just further down than you,' said Chloe modestly. 'You'd have noticed it too, I bet.'

'Maybe the gateway is really near us,' said Mistral in excitement.

'If it is here we have to get to it from below,' Erin remembered. 'That's what the diary says.'

Chloe flew into the air. Erin followed her and the two horses dissolved into their misty cloud form and cantered up into the sky. They all swooped over the cliff edge. The sea was still out.

'Look, there it is!' said Chloe, landing very carefully on the sharp rocks. She pointed to an overhanging ledge that was about two metres up the cliff. Erin landed beside her and saw a cave entrance underneath the ledge. It was made from a slab of rock and it hid the cave well. Erin looked inside. The cave was really dark and the floor was covered with pools of water.

'We have to go in,' she said. 'But it's so dark. We won't be able to see a thing. I wish we'd got a torch.'

'Hang on!' said Chloe. She raced up to the cliff top and returned with two fallen branches. 'Fire be with me,' she said, pointing her hands at the top of them. They burst into flame. Chloe handed one gingerly to Erin. 'I don't know how long they'll last, but they should help us for a little bit.'

Tor and Mistral backed away uneasily from the burning branches as bits of leaf and bark spat into the air.

'I'll go first if you like,' offered Chloe.

Erin hesitated. She didn't really *want* to lead the way, but she felt she should. 'No, it's OK.'

She stepped into the cave, holding the branch high so that the flames lit up the darkness. The walls were thrown into shadow, but straight away she could see a tunnel at the back. She walked towards it. The water on the floor was very cold under her feet. Goosebumps

prickled on her arms. She looked round and was relieved to see Tor shrinking slightly in size and following Chloe in, Mistral walking beside him.

Erin headed warily down the tunnel. The burning branch spat. Erin flinched and almost dropped it as a burning piece of bark touched her hand. She saw a dark hollow high up in the wall.

Holding the branch up, Erin found that a small white candle in a metal tray had been placed in the hollow. There was another one further on.

'There are candles!' she exclaimed in relief. She took one down. The wick seemed dry. They had been high enough that the sea hadn't reached them recently. 'Chloe! Can you light them?

It only took Chloe a few minutes to point her finger and light the candle and then put the branches out. The candles didn't give off much light, but it was better than the burning sticks and Erin felt somehow reassured by the little tea lights as they flickered in the darkness. Maybe her mum had left them there.

This has to be the way to the gateway, she realized. *Why else would there be candles here?*

She continued cautiously down the cold, dark tunnel wondering what they were going to find. What would the gateway be like? Where was it?

Chloe walked beside her, lighting every new candle they came across. After a few minutes they saw the end of the tunnel. Erin felt excitement leap inside her. It looked like it opened out into a small cave. Was that where they were going to find the gateway?

She and Chloe stepped into the cave with Tor and Mistral following. The ceiling was high up. Chloe held up one of the candles and they looked around. There were no tunnels leading off this cave. It was just a dead end. A round space with smooth walls, a high ceiling and nothing else.

For a moment none of them said anything.

'There's nothing here,' said Chloe at last.

Erin didn't know what she'd been expecting. Some sort of stone formation, a rock with a hole in it like the one that used to stand at World's End maybe. But Chloe was right, there was nothing that looked like a gateway.

'Maybe this isn't the place,' said Mistral uncertainly.

'But it has to be,' argued Erin. 'Otherwise why would the candles be here and it . . .' she struggled to explain, 'it just *feels* right.'

'Magic has been worked here,' Tor agreed.

'But there's no gateway, Father,' said Mistral.

'Hey, look! What's that,' said Chloe, pointing to a faint glimmering circle on the floor. 'It wasn't there a moment ago.'

They all stared at the circle. As they stared, it got brighter and brighter, a perfect round disc of light forming on the floor.

'The moon!' gasped Erin, looking up.

In the ceiling, way, way above them, there was a round hole, about thirty centimetres wide. Moonlight was streaming through it and making the circle of light on the floor. 'The cliff top must be up there,' realized Chloe.

Tor whinnied in excitement, the sound echoing loudly around the cave. '*Made from moonlight!*' He stamped a hoof. 'Don't you see? This is the gateway. It is a circle of moonlight!'

Erin gasped. 'Deep underground! Like the prophecy said. And I bet the whispering tree is probably just above us, near where the hole up there is!'

'We've found it!' Chloe exclaimed.

'Oh, Tor, we can set you and Mistral free now!'

But just as she spoke, clouds covered the moon in the skies and the gateway disappeared.

'We'll have to clear the skies of clouds, Erin, before we can use the gateway,' said Tor. 'We'll have to be quick though. The moon moves across the sky. It will only shine in the right place to create the gateway for a short time.'

But as Erin started to nod, there was a thundering and a rumbling from behind them.

'What's that?' said Chloe in alarm.

CRASH!

They all jumped as the whole cave seemed to shake. 'What just happened?' asked Erin.

But even Tor looked uncertain.

'Let's go and see,' said Chloe, her voice shaky.

'I'll go first.' Tor trotted past Chloe into the first cave. Erin heard him whinny in dismay.

She and Chloe stopped as they reached the cave. A large slab of rock now blocked the entrance. There were small spaces around the sides, but none of them were anywhere near big enough for the girls to get through.

'We're . . . we're trapped!' stammered Chloe.

From outside the cave, Erin heard a familiar laugh.

'Trapped and unable to do anything,' Marianne's cold voice said. 'You fools! You made it too easy for me. It was a small matter to break the ledge above the entrance. You will stay there while I create a dark gateway I can use to get to the cloud world. Now I have the diary it is, at last, possible for me to do the magic I need.'

Erin felt panic rising in her throat. 'You can't leave us here!'

Marianne's voice was silky-smooth. 'I most certainly can.'

'Let us out!' yelled Chloe, running over to the rock.

But there was no reply. Marianne had gone.

Eleven

'What are we going to do?' exclaimed Erin, staring at the slab of rock that was blocking the entrance.

Chloe looked round. 'What about the hole in the ceiling where the moonlight shines through? Could we get through that somehow?'

'It's too small!' Erin remembered how the sky horses could swirl into mist. 'You and Mistral would be able to get through it though, Tor.'

'But that would mean leaving you here,' said Tor.

Chloe's eyes lit up with an idea. 'Maybe you and Mistral could fly out, then you could scrape away the soil until the hole was big enough for us to get through.'

Tor nodded slowly. ' Yes, that would work.'

'But it would destroy the gateway,' protested Mistral.

'Then you can't do it. This is the only gateway left that we know about!' cried Erin. 'If we destroy it, you'll never get back to the sky.'

'We do not have a choice,' said Tor in a voice that would brook no argument. 'It is the only way. We have to get you out and then we have to stop Marianne.'

'What did she mean when she said she would make a dark gateway, Tor?' asked Chloe anxiously.

'It is a gateway made using dark magic,' Tor replied. 'It can only be used by the spirit who creates it. It gives that person complete access to the cloud world so they may come and go as they please.'

'But, if someone does that, doesn't it make the sky horses ill?' asked Erin, remembering what she had read in her mum's diary.

Tor nodded. 'Marianne will not care about that though – all she wants is power. In fact, if the herd is weakened, it will be easier to make them do as she pleases. I did not realize she would try this. To make a dark gateway she needs

to use the power of another weather
weaver.'

'My power?' said Erin.

Tor nodded. 'But not just yours. That
would not be enough on its own.' He
broke off. 'I should have realized what
she was really after. Did your mother
leave a lock of hair?'

'Yes,' said Erin in surprise. 'Why?'

Tor spoke heavily. 'Weather weavers usually do. Hair holds power in weather weaving. Marianne must have been after the diary because she wanted the lock of hair. You know that the magic of weather weavers who are related is linked? That the power from one adds to the power of the other. By using your mother's hair as well as one of your hairs to create the dark gateway, she will increase the power she can get from you.'

'But she hasn't got one of my hairs,' said Erin.

'She might have!' exclaimed Chloe in horror. 'Erin, do you remember that time we went to Marianne's house to find the binding stone when Tor was captured? We took the stone with

her hair on but left another stone
with three of your hairs on in its
place so Marianne wouldn't notice
her own stone was missing. Well,
when you broke the binding spell,
she must have realized her stone
had gone and I bet she would easily
have guessed the hair we left was
yours.'

Erin stared. She had almost forgotten
that.

'We must stop her before she starts
to make the dark gateway!' Tor turned
sharply to the colt, who was beside the
rock at the entrance. 'Come on,
Mistral.'

'Wait, Father!' said Mistral. 'Maybe I
can move this rock and then we
wouldn't have to destroy the hidden

gateway. Look!' He shimmered and changed to his solid form, then he pushed his shoulder against the rock. It moved a few centimetres. 'We might be able to push our way out.'

Erin and Chloe hurried over and added their strength to his. They leant against it, pushing with all their might. The rock moved a few more

centimetres and then refused to budge any more.

'This is useless!' said Chloe in frustration. 'If only you could push it with us, Tor, we'd be bound to be able to move it.'

But the cave was too small and low for the stallion to change into his solid form. Mistral's ears were almost touching the roof and he was much smaller than Tor.

'What are we going to do?' asked Erin.

Tor looked at the gaps. 'Maybe I *could* push it. Mistral, come with me!'

Tor's body lost its horse shape, dissolving into a stream of silvery mist that swirled out of one of the gaps at the side of the rock.

Mistral looked puzzled, but followed him, his body shimmering into mist too.

'What are they doing?' asked Chloe.

Erin didn't know, but it felt horrid being in the damp, dark cave completely on their own without the horses' company. 'Tor!' she called anxiously. 'Where have you gone?'

Tor whinnied from outside. 'Stand back! Mistral and I are going to try to push the rock inwards.'

'But it's really heavy,' said Erin.

The girls heard the clatter of hooves on stones and then the cloud horses began to push. The rock slowly began to edge into the cave. As the gaps between it and the wall grew larger, Erin saw Tor, his head lowered, his shoulder pushing, the muscles and veins under his skin standing out with the effort.

'Be careful!' begged Erin. The rock was heavy and she didn't want either of the horses to hurt themselves.

'It won't go any further!' whinnied Mistral as the rock got caught on a chunk of stone jutting out of the roof of the entrance.

'But we can't quite get out yet,' said Chloe. The gaps were just too narrow for either of them to squeeze through.

'We *will* move it!' Tor pushed with all his strength, forcing the rock against the stone spur in the roof. Suddenly there was a loud crack as it broke. At the same moment, the rock blocking the entrance rolled into the cave and the stone chunk fell down from the ceiling. Tor saw it coming and shied back out of the way, but he was too late. The pointed heavy stone crashed into his front right leg.

'Tor!' cried Erin in alarm. 'Are you all right?'

'Yes,' the stallion said. But he was holding his leg up and Erin could hear the pain in his voice.

'You're not! You're hurt!' She ran to the rock. The final push had left a gap wide enough for her to scramble through. She squeezed around the rock, hardly noticing as she grazed her arms and legs. Stumbling out of the cave, she stopped by Tor. 'Your leg,

Tor!' She crouched down as Chloe joined her. His leg was not bleeding, but she could tell from the way he was holding it up that it was causing him a lot of pain.

'Do not worry,' replied Tor, nuzzling her hair. 'It is injured, but it will heal in time.'

'Father! Look!' whinnied Mistral, staring at the top of the cliff. A dark-grey mist seemed to be swirling over the trees there.

'Marianne has started the spell,' said Tor. 'We must act now!'

He turned into his cloud form, limped forward a few paces and then plunged up into the sky. Once he was flying, he moved more easily. Mistral followed him. Erin and Chloe raced

after them. Erin pushed all the
questions that were racing around her
mind away. They had to stop
Marianne!

CHAPTER
Twelve

Tor and Mistral flew over the edge of the cliff with the girls following. Marianne was standing on the ground among the trees. She was holding a seeing stone in one hand, waving the other hand over it and muttering words that Erin could not hear. The dark mist swirled above the topmost branches. It was thick and grey and dense. It seemed to suck light from all around it.

Tor whinnied. 'Stop!'

'You!' Marianne swung round, looking momentarily shocked. 'How did *you* escape?'

'It is enough that we did,' Tor told her. 'We are here now and you will not open the dark gateway.'

'You cannot stop me.' Marianne gestured upwards at the mist. 'The magic has already begun.' Reaching into the pocket of her dress, she pulled out a blue leather-bound book. 'And it's all thanks to this! The power of the child was not enough, but with the power of her mother too . . .'

'So Tor was right, it wasn't the hidden gateway you needed the diary for!' cried Chloe. 'It was the hair!'

'That little pothole would never have given me the complete access to the clouds I need,' Marianne said. 'It can only be used when the tide is out and the moon is in the right place. It is next to useless.'

Erin stiffened. 'I want the diary. It's my mum's. Give it back!' She felt the air shift beside her, but her gaze was riveted on Marianne.

Marianne smiled. 'No. It is mine now.'

The next minute, Marianne was staggering back, the book gone. 'What –'

Chloe appeared in the air, flying away from her. The book was in her hands. She had camouflaged herself and swooped down on Marianne while the dark spirit was distracted talking to Erin! Chloe raced to Erin and thrust the book at her. 'Here!'

Erin gaped. Chloe had moved so fast!

For a moment Marianne looked
furious, but then she shrugged. 'You can
have it. I do not need it now anyway.
At last I am going to be able to control
the weather in the skies as I have always
dreamed of.'

Erin clutched the diary. 'No, you
won't. We'll stop you!'

'You!' laughed Marianne. 'Even my

sister at the peak of her strength only just managed to stop me last time. How could a child like you stand in my way?'

Erin stared at her. 'What do you mean?'

Marianne smiled. 'Oh, Erin, I know you've been trying to figure it out because I've been watching you these last few weeks, listening in to your conversations. You want to know how we are related, don't you?'

'Yes.' The word escaped Erin before she could stop it.

Marianne's blue eyes met hers. 'You think I am called Marianne. But my real name is May. I am your great-grandmother's sister.'

Erin vaguely heard Chloe's astonished gasp and Tor's surprised snort.

'May?' Erin echoed in astonishment 'But . . . but you can't be. You're not old enough.'

Marianne smiled. 'That is the power of dark magic, Erin. You know this face –' she pointed to herself – 'but now see my real one.' She waved a hand once in front of her and started to change. Her smooth, unlined skin collapsed into wrinkles, her eyes sank deep into her face, her body shrank, her long blonde hair became grey and wispy, her fingers curled like claws. She looked ancient. Her eyes glittered and she laughed at Erin, who instinctively shrank closer to Tor.

Venomous words hissed out of Marianne's mouth. 'Your great-grandmother was my oh-so-*wonderful* older sister who everyone adored. Always telling me what to do, always lecturing me when I wanted more power. I could have had complete control over the weather, but no – she wouldn't let me. She forced me to let the stallion I had captured go, but then I waited. And as she got old I used my magic to stay young until the moment came when I could try again. That time is now and you will not stop me, my great-great-niece. No one will. I am finally going to get what I have been waiting for. The skies are finally going to be mine!'

She turned, held up the hagstone in her hand and screamed out: 'Begin!'

The mist swirled downwards like a tornado and then streamed towards the stone in her hand.

Tor plunged forward. Mistral too. They galloped towards Marianne. But they were too late to stop it. The mist was already flowing through the stone. It formed a perfect circle that hovered in the air.

'The dark gateway!' hissed Marianne in triumph. As the sky horses landed, she suddenly began to change shape, her neck lengthened, her arms became legs . . .

'Erin! She's turning into a horse!' cried Chloe.

Before the words were even out of Chloe's mouth, Marianne had transformed into a coal-black horse with blazing eyes. She leapt at Mistral, ears flattened. The foal had no time to react. The black horse's teeth raked down his shoulder before it squealed and swung round, rising on to its hind legs to clash with Tor, who had galloped over to protect his son. Their forelegs struck out. But Erin saw that Tor could hardly use his left one.

One of the black horse's hooves sliced his good shoulder. The other landed a savage blow on his injured leg. Tor staggered back to the ground.

Mistral lunged furiously at the black horse again, but it was already swinging round. Erin saw its muscles bunch and then it leapt upwards through the dark gateway.

The gateway and the horse disappeared. There was nothing. Just empty air and silence.

Chloe stared. 'She's gone.'

'Yes, to my cloud world,' said Tor grimly, 'where she will try to take control of the herd.'

Erin thought about the storms that would come, the flooding, the lightning – the danger. 'She's won!' she said in despair.

'No, she hasn't,' Tor responded.

Mistral stared at him. 'But what can we do, Father? She'll use her dark gateway to come and go as she pleases and that will make the herd ill. Erin's right. She has won.'

Tor lifted his head and looked at the skies. 'All is not lost yet. We *can* still stop her.'

'How?' demanded Chloe.

'By going through the hidden gateway and bringing her back,' Tor

answered. 'Then Erin can use her magic
to destroy her dark gateway and
afterwards seal the hidden one under
the ground so that neither Marianne
nor anyone else can ever pass between
the worlds again. We *can* do it.' His dark
eyes flashed. 'Marianne may have won
this time, but we are still strong and
we can still fight. She has not defeated
us yet.'

Erin felt hope fill her. 'No, she
hasn't!' She looked around at the others.
'We're not going to give up, are we?'

'Of course not!' said Chloe, and
Mistral whinnied in agreement.

'We'll bring her back and seal the
gateway,' Erin told Tor, putting a hand
on his neck.

Tor nuzzled her, and Erin gazed at

the stars glittering in the velvet-black
sky. The night looked so peaceful, but
she knew that out there Marianne was
waiting. The storm was still to come . . .

Discover magical new worlds with
Linda Chapman

⭐ **Gallop** with the unicorns at Unicorn Meadows

⭐ **Fly** with the magical spirits of Stardust Forest

⭐ **Swim** through Mermaid Falls with Electra and her friends

⭐ **Play** with new friends at Unicorn School

With great **activities**, gorgeous **downloads**, games galore and an exciting new **online fanzine!**

What are you waiting for?
The magic begins at

lindachapman.co.uk

It all started with a Scarecrow

Puffin is well over sixty years old.
Sounds ancient, doesn't it? But Puffin has never been
so lively. We're always on the lookout for the next big
idea, which is how it began all those years ago.

Penguin Books was a big idea from the mind of
a man called Allen Lane, who in 1935 invented
the quality paperback and changed the world.
**And from great Penguins, great Puffins grew,
changing the face of children's books forever.**

The first four Puffin Picture Books were hatched in 1940 and the
first Puffin story book featured a man with broomstick arms called
Worzel Gummidge. In 1967 Kaye Webb, Puffin Editor, started the
Puffin Club, promising to **'make children into readers'**.
She kept that promise and over 200,000 children became
devoted Puffineers through their quarterly instalments of
Puffin Post, which is now back for a new generation.

Many years from now, we hope you'll look back and
remember Puffin with a smile. **No matter what your age
or what you're into, there's a Puffin for everyone.**
The possibilities are endless, but one thing is for sure:
whether it's a picture book or a paperback, a sticker book
or a hardback, **if it's got that little Puffin
on it – it's bound to be good.**